C0-AMO-876

This book belongs to:

....

....

....

Retold by Gaby Goldsack
Illustrated by Ruth Galloway (Advocate)
Designed by Jester Designs

Language consultant: Betty Root

ISBN 0-75259-431-1

This is a P³ book
This edition published 2002

P³
Queen Street House
4 Queen Street
Bath BA1 1HE, UK

Copyright © Exclusive Editions 2002

Printed in China.

All rights reserved. No part of this publication may be reproduced,
stored in a retrieval system, or transmitted by any means,
mechanical, photocopying, recording or otherwise, without
the prior permission of the copyright holder.

p^3

The Ugly Duckling

Helping your Child Read

Learning to read is an exciting challenge for most children. From a very early age, sharing story books with children, talking about the pictures, and guessing what might happen next are all very important parts of the reading experience.

Sharing reading

Set aside a regular quiet time to share reading with younger children, or to be on hand to encourage older children as they develop into independent readers.

First Readers are intended to encourage and support the early stages of learning to read. They present well-loved tales that children will enjoy hearing again and again. Familiarity helps children to identify some of the words and phrases.

When you feel your child is ready to move ahead, encourage him or her to join in so that you read the story aloud together. Always pause to talk about the pictures. The easy-to-read speech bubbles in **First Readers** provide an excellent "joining-in" activity. The bright, clear illustrations and matching text will help children to understand the story.

Building confidence

In time, children will want to read *to* you. When this happens, be patient and give continual praise. They may not read all the words correctly, but children's substitutions are often good guesses.

The repetition in each book is particularly helpful for building confidence. If your child cannot read a particular word, go back to the beginning of the sentence and read it together so the meaning is not lost. Most importantly, do not continue if your child is tired or just needs a change.

Reading alone

The next step is for your child to read alone. Try to be available to give help and support. Remember to give lots of encouragement and praise.

Together with other simple stories, **First Readers** will help ensure reading is an enjoyable and rewarding experience.

One day a mother duck sat on her nest.
She was waiting for her eggs to hatch.

She waited and waited.

Then, crack! They started to hatch.

crack!

Out popped three fluffy yellow ducklings.

Now there was just one egg left. It was a very big egg. The mother duck sat back down.

Come on, hatch!

She waited and waited. She thought it would never hatch.

Then, crack! It started to hatch.

Out popped a big gray duckling.

The gray duckling looked big and ugly.

The mother duck took her new ducklings
down to the pond. She showed them
how to swim.

Soon they could all swim.

Even the big gray duckling.

The mother duck was
very pleased.

The mother duck took her new
ducklings up to the farm.

All the animals thought the gray
duckling was ugly.

"What an ugly duckling!" they said.

So the ugly duckling ran away.

He ran to the other side of the pond.
Wild ducks lived on the other side of
the pond.

The wild ducks thought the gray
duckling was ugly.

"What an ugly duckling!" they said.

So the ugly duckling ran away.

He ran to a cottage. An old woman lived in the cottage. She lived with a cat and a hen.

The cat and the hen thought the big duckling was ugly.

"What an ugly duckling!" they said.

So the ugly duckling ran away.

He ran to the lake.

One day he saw some swans fly by.

They were beautiful.

"I wish I looked like that,"
said the ugly duckling.

Winter came. It grew colder and colder.

The lake turned to ice.

The ugly duckling got stuck in the ice.

A farmer found him.

He took him home.

The farmer's children wanted to play with the ugly duckling. The ugly duckling was frightened.
So the duckling ran away.

He ran back to the pond.

He stayed there until spring.

The sun came out. The ugly duckling flapped his wings. They felt strong.

He flapped and flapped until he was flying high in the air.

The ugly duckling flew back to the lake.

He saw three beautiful swans on the lake.

The ugly duckling landed on the lake. He looked at himself in the lake.

He was not an ugly duckling.
He was a beautiful swan.

"Be our friend!" said the other swans.

The ugly duckling had some friends
at last.

Read and Say

How many of these words can you say?
The pictures will help you. Look back in
your book and see if you can find the
words in the story.

cat

hen

cottage

duck

ducklings

eggs

farmer

farm

pond

swans

Titles in this series: